I Can't, I Won't
No Way!

A Book for Children Who Refuse to Poop

By Tracey Vessillo
Illustrations by MikeMotz.com

This book was inspired by,
and is dedicated to my daughter, Olivia.
My greatest gift in this world...
My greatest gift to this world.

I Can't, I Won't, No Way!
A Book for Children Who Refuse to Poop

Story by Tracey Vessillo
Illustrations by MikeMotz.com

ISBN: 1466453737
EAN-13: 978-1466453739

Printed in the U.S.A.

I Can't, I Won't No Way!

According to recent studies, more than 1 in 5 healthy children struggle with the challenges of bowel withholding, "encopresis." Among this category, eighty percent are stool toileting refusers whose behavior lasts more than six months. Parents and children alike experience a sense of isolation due to a lack of support and limited resources.

"I Can't, I Won't, No Way!" written by Tracey J. Vessillo, brings a combination of compassion and humor to her creation of a warm and touching story. A must have for parents and children coping with the intensity of bowel withholding.

Drawing from personal experience, Tracey's keen awareness of psychology and parenting affords her the opportunity to share a compassionate and supportive view.

This book can be a critical tool for both parents and children attempting to navigate their way through one of the most frustrating aspects of the toilet training process.

Earl Rectanus, Ph.D.
Licensed Psychologist

I know that I should sit to poop.

But I believe that I must stand.

One day in the potty,
my poops they will just land.

My mom and dad, they try to help,
but I refuse to go.

What I am afraid of?
I'm not even sure I know.

Why do poops have to change?
They never seem just right.

One day they sink, one day they float,
I squeeze my butt so tight.

My mom says, "Let them out, you won't have any pain."

I'm getting very grouchy.
I can't! I won't! No way!

Let me think of something else.
I'll hold them one more day.

I hide where I can't be found
until my poops they just fall out.

Have patience with me, Mom and Dad;
I can't stand to see you pout.

I'm not sure why this is;
I'll go at my own pace.

I know I'm getting older,
but it's really not a race.

I'm sorry that it seems
I do nothing more than cry!

Then one day it happened,
much to my surprise!

I sat down on the potty,
and they appeared before my eyes.

Now I poop every day.
I understand it's no big deal.

Finally! I can't believe how much better I do feel.

So, for all you children out there who believe that you can't poop.

Just sit right down and relax,
promise you will try.

Let the poops fall right out,
then flush and wave good-bye.

You will be proud
(and your mom and dad, of course).

When you know without a doubt,
of your poops you are the boss!

Made in the USA
San Bernardino, CA
10 July 2019